Olaf Waits for Spring

By Victoria Saxon
Illustrated by the Disney Storybook Art Team

 A GOLDEN BOOK • NEW YORK

rhcbooks.com
ISBN 978-0-7364-3765-3 (trade) — ISBN 978-0-7364-3917-6 (ebook)
Printed in the United States of America
10 9 8 7 6 5 4 3

One chilly morning, Olaf found his friends preparing to travel up into the mountains.

"Hi, Kristoff! Hi, Sven!" Olaf said. "What are you doing?"

"It's almost spring, so I have to check on my ice-harvesting equipment," Kristoff replied.

"Spring?" Olaf cried. "What about summer? I just *looove* summer!"

"Spring comes before summer," said
Kristoff. "And spring is amazing, too.
We can go sailing! Just wait and see!"

"Maybe I'll love spring as much as summer," Olaf said as he headed inside the castle. "But I don't know. . . ."

Elsa was talking to Olina. "In the spring, we'll have fresh fruit, and with fruit, we can make pie," said Olina.

"Ooh, I love pie!" Olaf said. "Uh, what's pie?"

Elsa smiled. "It's a delicious dessert. Just wait and see."

Olaf raced outside to find Anna.

"Spring is coming soon," he cried. "With sailing and pies!"

"Ah, I love spring," Anna said. "That's when crocuses bloom and all the cute baby animals are born. Just wait and see!"

Olaf was excited. "I'm going to find
the best place to wait for spring!" he told
himself. And off he went!

Olaf walked and walked. He wanted to find a place where he would see all the boats and pies and crocuses and baby animals when they arrived.

Finally, he settled on a spot high on a mountain. And he waited.

But the only thing that arrived was a snowstorm.

"Hmm," said Olaf. "This is not quite how I imagined springtime."

Then he saw something far in the distance. "Oh!" he gasped. "Are those spring babies?"

Olaf ran toward the babies—only to discover that they were actually his friends.

"Olaf!" Anna exclaimed. "We've been looking all over for you!"

"I was just on the mountaintop, waiting," Olaf said.

"Waiting for what?" asked Anna.

"For spring, of course!" he replied. "Just like you all told me to. I'm so excited that it's almost here!"

"Because as soon as it arrives, we'll go sailing . . ."

"... and enjoy fresh pies and colorful crocuses ..."

". . . and best of all, greet the spring babies!"

"Olaf," Elsa said gently, "spring doesn't arrive all at once. It's gradual."

"Sailing can be difficult at the beginning of spring," said Kristoff, "because there's still ice in the fjord. First the ice melts and bigger ships come in and out of the fjord." He smiled. "It might be a while before it's warm enough for us to go sailing in a smaller boat."

"And it doesn't get warm overnight,"
Anna added as they walked toward town.
"Look in that tree," Elsa said. "The
birds are preparing for their babies."

"Do you see the nest, Olaf?" Anna asked. "First comes the nest, then the eggs. After that, the baby birds will hatch."

"Remember how Olina talked about making pies?" said Elsa. "Well, right now the sun is melting the snow. The ground will get muddy, but soon fresh fruits, vegetables, and crocuses will begin to grow."

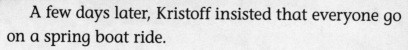

A few days later, Kristoff insisted that everyone go on a spring boat ride.

"This is only the beginning of spring. It will get warmer soon, and then we'll be able to go for longer sails," Anna told Olaf as she huddled under a blanket next to Kristoff. "It just takes time."

"That's okay," said the little snowman. "I love waiting for spring!"

As it turned out, Olaf didn't have to wait very long. In only a few weeks, spring was popping up everywhere.

"Ohhh," he sighed. "Summer is great, but you know what? I love spring, too!"